Before he could take one step, Mrs Morris came running towards him.

"Oh PC Button!" she cried

"Marmalade has got himself stuck up a tree and won't come down".

He quickly climbed the tree and got Marmalade down safely.

PC Button was now covered in twigs, leaves and moss.

"I should call you PC Scarecrow," laughed Mrs Morris.

Next stop was the vet's, where Mr Paws was hard at work painting a new sign.

Just as PC Button said good morning a gust of wind wobbled the ladder, and Mr Paws let go of the paint pot. It landed right on top of PC Buttons helmet.

"Whoops!" called Mr Paws.

"Accidents will happen!"

PC Button drove along the road to Goosefeather Farm,
covered in twigs, leaves and bright red paint.
He was feeling rather grumpy.
"What a sight!" laughed Farmer Shepherd.
The animals, however, were so shocked by the way he
looked that they ran away as fast as they could, covering
PC Button in mud from head to toe.

PC Button drove back to the village, feeling dirty cold and wet.

"What has happened to you?" asked Petula as he got out of the car.

Before he could answer, he felt a tickle in his nose, and he began to sneeze.

"Aiitchoooooooooo!"

The sneeze was so loud that it shook all the petals from the flowers on Petula's stall.

Oh dear! They landed in a big pile on PC Button's head!

Passing the Baker's Shop, PC Button decided to pop in for his favourite sticky bun.

"That will cheer me up no end," he said, licking his lips.

However, his wet boots made him slip and slide across the bakery floor.

He knocked into Mr Bun, who was carrying a huge tray of cherry pies to the oven.

PC Button was covered in flour, and a big red cherry landed on his nose!

"You look like a clown!" laughed Mr Bun.

Back at home, PC Button felt very sorry for himself, as he began to iron the creases in his trousers.

Just then, there was a knock at the door. PC Button's frown turned into a smile.

"We thought you needed cheering up," called Mrs Morris. Behind her stood the whole of HappyLand Village, with cakes, lemonade....and washing powder.

But, what was that burning smell?

PC Button had left the iron on his uniform trousers, and there was a big hole in the knee.

"Looks like I'll be wearing shorts from now on!" laughed PC Button.

THE END!

Mr Leek   Petula   Postman Percy   Mrs Morris   Reverend Hughes

Mr Barley   Mrs Barley   Charlie   Poppy   PC Button

Farmer Shepherd   Mrs Shepherd   Delia   Mr Bun   Granny Bonnet